D0856150

ADVENTURE TIME Volume One
ISBN: 9781782760009

Published by Titan Comics, a division of Titan Publishing Group Ltd., 144 Southwark St., London, SE1 0UP. Contains material originally published in single comic form as ADVENTURE TIME 1-4 & ADVENTURE TIME FREE COMIC BOOK DAY EDITION. © Cartoon Network. (S12) All rights reserved. All characters, events and institutions depicted herein are fictional. Any similarity between any of the names, characters, persons, events and/or institutions in this publication and actual names, characters and persons, whether living or dead, and/or institutions are unintended and purely coincidental.

A CIP catalogue record for this title is available from the British Library.

Printed in China.

First published: November 2012
8 10 9 7

We love to hear from our readers. Please email us at: readercomments@titanemail.com, or write to us at the above address. For all the latest news, information, competitions and exclusive offers, sign up to our latest newsletter at:
www.titan-comics.com

CREATED BY
Pendleton Ward

WRITTEN BY
Ryan North

ILLUSTRATED BY
Shelli Paroline and Braden Lamb

"BMO'S LESSON"
ILLUSTRATED BY
Mike Holmes
COLORS BY STUDIO PARLAPÁ

LETTERS BY
Steve Wands

COVER BY
Chris Houghton
COLORS BY KASSANDRA HELLER

EDITOR
Shannon Watters

ASSISTANT EDITOR
Adam Staffaroni

TRADE DESIGN & "BMO IN THE DESERT" ILLUSTRATIONS BY
Stephanie Gonzaga

"BMO IN THE DESERT" COLORS BY
KASSANDRA HELLER

With special thanks to
Marisa Marionakis, Rick Blanco, Curtis Lelash, Laurie Halal-Ono, Keith
Mack, Kelly Crews and the wonderful folks at Cartoon Network.

ADVENTURE TIME

Jake the Dog: Magical dog with stretchy powers. Pal rating at 110%!

Finn the Human: Awesome dude with awesome hat. Pal rating at 110%!

The Land of Ooo: A pretty magical place! Jake and Finn live here. Adventure possibility: **UNLIMITED??**

Really good at being pals **AND** at adventures!

Ice King: All he wants to do is marry a princess, and he thinks stealing them is okay!

The Lich: **HE IS COMING.**

Marceline the Vampire Queen: Over a thousand years old. Be cool, okay?

Princess Bubblegum: Human/bubblegum ruler of the Candy Kingdom. She's made of gum! She and Finn are friends, and sometimes feelings can get complicated, you know?

Not as important as the other boxes, just a heads up.

Written by **Ryan North** Art by **Shelli Paroline** and **Braden Lamb** "Adventure Time" created by **Pendleton Ward**

BMO runs on electricity and likes taking nice pictures!

Not pictured is the **EARL OF LEMONGRAB**, who is currently sitting in a chair in an empty room, screaming.

KCCCHT

Uh oh.

OH DANG! WE'LL GET BACK TO THE LICH,
BUT FIRST IN ANOTHER PART OF OOO...

BMO'S LESSON!

WITH

JAKE   FINN   BUBBLEGUM   BMO

"THE DOG"   "THE HUMAN"   "THE PRINCESS"   "THE COMPUTER"

I want to be the best BMO I can be, Princess! I want to be the best BMO.

You are the best BMO!

No, because sometimes, I have made little mistakes.

Aw, we all make mistakes!

PFFFT

See? I make mistakes too: I grabbed the wrong milk. This isn't from cows!

You... drink from cows?

Yeah, sometimes.

But I am a computer, Princess! I was programmed to be perfect.

...I think?

Well, what do you want to be perfect at?

I WANT TO BE PERFECT AT FIGHTS!!

SOON:

Thanks for joining us, Finn and Jake!

Not a problem! We're always ready to help out.

We're easy to the peasy!

Okay. I think we should start training with punches.

Hi-yah!

Not bad! But you also need to know how to block a punch thrown at you. Boys?

Jake, I'm going to punch you but it's just for pretend!

Finn, I'm going to block your punch but it doesn't mean we're not still ULTIMATE SUPER-BROS!

Here come a bunch of good reasons and one smaller but still good reason why you're gonna get hurt!!

He's referring to his fingers and thumb!

Whoah! Jake! NICE!

Thanks! But watch out, buddy, because that compliment is going straight to my...

...HEAD!

Ha ha ha!

That was awesome, dude.

Heh. I thought you might like it!

But Jake, I can't do crazy messed up things with my head like that!

That's true. Jake, can you fight without your powers?

I dunno. Probably?

No powers! No powers!

Okay Finn, punch me again! I won't use my powers when I block it, honest.

Here it comes!

PUNCH

OW OW OW OW OW OW OW!

That!
Was!
AWESOME!

My turn!
My turn!

You sure? You only saw it once, that might not be enough to learn everything there is about flipping du--

I am a COMPUTER, Finn!

Okay, okay! Here comes the punch, BMO!

rrrrr...

Am I the best at fighting yet??

Maybe physical fighting isn't your thing, BMO! There are other ways you can fight: passive-aggressively, intellectually, with words, or--

Words! BMO can fight with words!!

BMO can fight with BATTLE BURNS.

What are battle burns?

I will teach you! Try to punch me!

Okay!

Battle burns are when you're punching me and I say...

ahem

CENSORED DUE TO BMO'S BATTLE BURN BEING SO GOOD, IT CAN'T LEGALLY BE RELEASED TO THE GENERAL PUBLIC!!

BMO, THAT WAS AMAZING!

Nice!

My mind, she is blown!

Can you teach us... battle burns??

I'd love to use them at the royal court!!

SOON:

To do a battle burn, you need to think of the punches you'd like to punch, and then turn them all into words instead!

You mean up in my brain? I mean, up in my skull walnut?

Correct, Finn!

Hmm...

No punching...

Your sense of style is disagreeable to my aesthetic tastes.

This is hard, BMO!

Is it like when I'm punching someone's head off so it flies up into the sky, and I say something like "Heads up"? Or "Here, I'll give you a HEAD START"?

No! No Finn, that's not a burn at all! Those are puns, that's totally different!

I can see this is going to take a lot of work.

LATER:

Thanks for teaching us all about battle burns, BMO! I'm sure they'll come in handy.

You need to keep practicing! Tomorrow morning!

I know!

And I will keep practicing my body slams too. When you fall asleep tonight I am going to try to body slam you, Finn!

Awesome.

This has been a really wonderful weekend.

It has, hasn't it? I don't think anything could happen now to ruin it.

It is not possible for ANYTHING and/or ANYONE to ruin this weekend, dude!

ELSEWHERE:

THIS IS TOO EASY.

Uncool, Lich.

You know what we gotta do, buddy...

Found them!

Asymptotic!

Slant asymptotic, dude!

I knew it was cool for a dude to keep anti-mind-control jewelry around the house.

Man, you know I don't judge. I kinda like wearing jewelry too sometimes.

We can talk about that later...

...because right now we've got an **EVIL LICH** to beat!!

Whoa!

He's headed towards the Candy Kingdom! **WE'VE GOT TO SAVE PRINCESS BUBBLEGUM!**

And everyone else who lives there too!

We've got to slow him down! Use a battle burn!

HEY, *LICH*! YOUR HANDS ARE SO *SKELETON*-Y AND *GROSS* THAT I BET NOBODY *EVER* WANTS TO HOLD YOUR HAND! I BET THAT MAKES YOU FEEL *BAD* WHEN YOU REALLY THINK ABOUT IT!!

I think you hurt his feelings, dude!

Totally worth it!!

BUMP!

FOOLS. I WILL SUCK EVERYTHING YOU'VE EVER KNOWN INTO THIS BAG AND THEN I WILL THROW IT INTO THE SUN. DO YOU REALLY THINK A BOY AND HIS BLOBBY DOG CAN STOP ME?

Yeah, we do!

THEN WATCH. WATCH AS YOUR PLANET DIES.

NEVER!

This is serious, dude. This is a real end-of-the-world scenario. I think we both know what we have to...nay, GET to do.

I hear you, man. Let's DO THIS!

Ready?

Ready!

JAAAAAAKE SUUUUUUUUUUUIT!

Have you tried **NOT** sucking for a change, Lich?!

KA-

POW

HA HA HA!

What are you laughing for? I punched you into two pieces!

And you should quit now, while you're A HEAD!

BUMP!

I DON'T THINK I WILL.

LOOK:

YOU'RE WASTING YOUR TIME.

PRINCESS BUBBLEGUM!

And everyone else who lives there tooooo!

AND NOW, YOU.

NO!

NOOOOOOOOOO!

I don't think he can hear us in here, dude.

Where are we?! Where's the way out? The Lich's butt isn't going to kick itself!

WE NEED TO HELP IT DO THAT, JAKE!!

Huh.

Maybe she knows?

Gentlemen! Hello!

Hello, your highness! I'm Jake the Dog, and this is my friend, Finn the Human. We're going to stop The Lich! He's uh, a skeleton dude. I think? It's gross. I dunno.

He's a gross jerk!!

I think we may have something in common, gentlemen, for it was THAT VERY SAME GROSS JERK who sent me here! Greetings Finn and Jake, and welcome to my kingdom.

I'm Desert Princess.

And it is very nice to meet you!!

SHAKE
SHAKE
SHAKE
SHAKE
SHAKE

THE LAND OF Ooo:

YES.

EVERYTHING IS GOING PERFECTLY.

The Lich!

Marceline's house!

What now?

INSIDE THE LICH'S BAG!

Man, if we don't find a way out soon the entire world is doomed!

We really should've saved the day by now, Jake.

Maybe this **IS** our world now, buddy. We could live right here!

You know... settle down, make ourselves a nice sand house to live in--no! A sand **CASTLE!** After all, Desert Princess lives here and she does all right.

Yes sir!

How long did you say you've lived here, DP?

I can't rightly say, Mister Finn! My earliest memory is of being sucked up by the Lich near some sort of...Candied Kingdom.

Hmm.

But it's blurry...**ALMOST** like I saw it from several different perspectives at once, as a bunch of candy citizens were smooshed together to form a new entity! But ha ha that's crazy!

Hmm...

Then I woke up here! Anyone as fancy as me is **CLEARLY** a princess, and I realized this has got to be my kingdom!

HMM...!

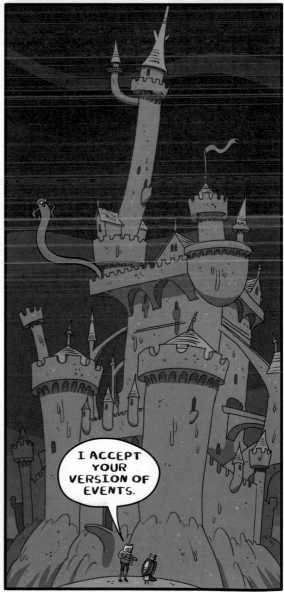

I ACCEPT YOUR VERSION OF EVENTS.

Desert Princess is as mysterious as she is...made out of desserts.

If we just pick a direction and run, we're bound to hit the edge of the bag eventually!!

SCIENCE.

Yes!

TWENTY MINUTES LATER:

Man, I'm pooped. I don't think running is the answer here, dudes. I think running--I think running might actually be the worst.

Gentlemen! Maybe we're thinking too two-dimensionally! Maybe we can escape...up?

Anything's better than runnninnnggggg

Remember when the Lich was attacking me and my totally sweet house?

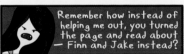

Remember how instead of helping me out, you turned the page and read about Finn and Jake instead?

Well I don't have to remember because he's still attacking me and IT'S HAPPENING RIGHT NOW!!

As soon as I get out of here, **SOMEONE**'s gonna get their butt kicked!

Obvs!

Who's there?! Hynden, is that you?

No, Marceline, it's me.

Wow. Way to dress, Bonnibel.

Royal dresses are too warm for the beach! Don't be mean!

So, you know a way off this island?

Maybe. What else can you turn into, besides bats and wolves and monsters?

I can also turn into a tentacle monster.

HOW DOES THAT HELP OUR SITUATION?

HOW DOES IT HURT OUR SITUATION, THOUGH?

ELSEWHERE IN THE BAG:

Dude! I didn't find a way out, but I **DID** see the Ice King nearby!! You wanna go mess with him?

He might know a way out of here!

Yeah, we should probably go mess with him.

Hey! Stop whatever you're doing!!

Oh, hey guys. You got bagged too, huh? It's pretty sucky here, am I right?

Ice King! You're evil, and I'm pretty sure you know a way out of here!

Hey, great to see you too, **FRIEND.** Look, I got nothing to do with this. I got sucked up just like everyone else, only I landed alone without Gunter **OR** my fan fiction.

Aw, that's awful. Hi there--I'm Desert Princess.

Thank you! Nice to get some empathy for once. These two only give me punches all up in my face.

Is that true?

He deserves it a lot of the time.

Is **THAT** true?

SHRUG

"Greetings, Jake!!" said cake, stretching herself to form the words "Greetings, Jake!!"

Ice King, if you wouldn't mind?

My pleasure, Princess.

Sure you don't want a sand-cheese and sand-cucumber sand-wich, Finn?

Naw, I'm good.

Your loss, dude.

Do you guys know why Gunter and my fictions didn't land here with me?

Nope! You're actually the first person we've seen here, besides Desert Princess.

Maybe we should ask why YOU landed so close to US!

Hmm...

Maybe--maybe it's because I'm... JOINED with you guys somehow? Our destinies somehow COSMICALLY INTER-TWINED?

Nuh-uh! If that were true then how come Princess Bubblegum or Flame Princess isn't here too?

I dunno, man. I think that's a question only your heart can answer.

My... heart?

Gross!!

Jeez Finn, be a little polite.

I personally find this lunch delicious, Desert Princess!

Thank you, Mr. King.

Look, Ice King, help us escape this bag! Remember that the Lich wants to destroy the entire world, **INCLUDING** all the princesses.

Princesses, shmincesses! A man my age has interests other than princesses, you know! Besides, **THIS** one doesn't want to marry me.

D-Do you?

No, thank you. I'm already married.

I'm not actually married, but it seemed the easiest way to let him down.

I should stress that I'm fully capable of living my life without a husband.

YEAH. ME TOO.

MEANWHILE, OUTSIDE THE BAG:

I can't even believe I used to live here, Melissa. I could just **DIE**.

Everything's gross here. You have to promise not to tell Brad I ever lived like this.

OH MY GLOB Melissa I gotta go!

There's this skeleton guy and he's sucking up all my stuff! I'm serious Melissa, he's sucking up my **LUMPING HOUSE!**

No I don't know him, Melissa. **NO!** No way I'm asking him that, **MELISSA.** I'm telling you, he's gross. **HE'S GROSS!**

Crust

Upper mantle

Mantle

Earth's outer core (liquid nickel and iron)

Bad news for every living thing on the planet

ALMOST DONE.

ARRRRGGGH!

I, THE TALKY ONE, REGRET TALKING SO MUCH.

Melissa? **MELISSA!** Skeleton guy made me say all that junk!

Zero bars?! I hate this lumping phone!

SPLAT

Hey there, guys.

Ugh.

Dudes, we're not making any progress on saving the world here!! In fact, we're making **NEGATIVE** progress, because now Lumpy Space Princess is here and all we've done is **HAVE A PICNIC!**

Though it was very nice of you to make it for us, Desert Princess.

I made the ice!

Thank you.

What do you want us to do, man? We've looked on the ground **AND** in the sky! There's nowhere else to look, unless somehow we could tunnel through the ground itself with some sort of amazing d--

AMAZING DRILL HANDS!!

To be fair, it's extremely hard NOT to hate a lumping phone with zero bars.

BUMP

Are you sure that doesn't hurt?

Aw, I'll be fine. This actually feels kinda good! I feel free, you know?

Whoa! I think we hit something!

KCHUNK

We hit bag!

SOON:

Desert Princess, I know we've just met, but Jake and I are going to go save the planet now. You three stay behind here, okay? Just in case.

In case of what?

Don't worry: Jake and I have come up with a REALLY TERRIFIC PLAN. But, should something go wrong, which is really unlikely, we need you guys to save the entire world without us, okay?

O--Okay.

And if something DOES go wrong, which again, I can barely conceive of happening, don't just, you know, wait a month before you save us.

Got it.

LUMPIN' SAVE THE WORLD ALREADY!

How come the tunnel is lit when there's no torches? It's the same way the inside of the bag is lit when there's no sun: SCIENCE. Wait no hold on wait wait I meant to say MAGIC.

Where?

Over there! But we're not gonna get there if you're not the sail.

Fine, jeez. Bossy much?

Marcy, I'm the SKIPPER.

SOON:

I could use some help!

SORRY! TOO BUSY BEING THE SAIL HERE, SKIP!

What do you think Finn and Jake are up to?

Aw, they're probably beating bad guys up as we speak. I'm sure we've got nothing to worry about.

What the cabbage?

PRINCESS BUBBLEGUM! PRINCESS BUBBLEGUM!! OH MY GLOB IT'S TERRIBLE! IT'S SO SAD!

Ladies, I don't really know how to say this, but...well--

FINN AND JAKE ARE TOTALLY DEAD!!

HA HA HA YES!

Thank you for going on this journey with us! This is...

The End

with Finn & Jake

was
Written by Ryan North
Art was done by Shelli Paroline and Braden Lamb
was Lettered by Steve Wands
"Adventure Time" created by Pendleton Ward

We're not dead!

WHAT'S UP, JERK?!?

OH SNAP! Not even a little bit!!

I was going to make this and all the remaining pages in the book entirely black and have the last page say "Hey, didn't you read page sixty. It's over!" but then Jake and Finn burst out of the bag. They saved both the day *AND* the quality of this comic!

Sorry we're late! Here's the KNUCKLE SANDWICH you ordered!

I DIDN'T--

I meant it METAPHORICALLY!!

PUNCH PUNCH

What have you done with Ooo? Why are we in space?!

PUNCH PUNCH

TELL HIM, JAKE.

Um...I think he really did suck up the entire planet into his bag?

YES.

AND ALL THAT REMAINS IS THIS LAST...

Hey! Don't say "little"!

...LITTLE...

If you say "bit" I'm coming back to kick your butt! I'ma shoot missiles in your face; I'm not even joking!

...BIT.

Those gemstones Finn and Jake are wearing also allow them to magically breathe and talk in space! This feature wasn't mentioned before because there's always been lots of air around, so it just never came up. You might even be wearing clothes that allow you to magically breathe and talk in space right now! *HOW WOULD YOU KNOW?*

Alternate, worse line for Princess Bubblegum: "That's okay, it's PLANE what's going on!" (because of Jet Jake) (did you know: not all puns are good?!)

Jet Jake moves in space the same way spaceships move in space: by expelling gas (i.e. toots)

That didn't go nearly as well as it did in my imagination.

Tell me about it, man! In my imagination his head exploded.

Listen, can you do me a favor on the way down? Think of a way we can beat him while he's got that stupid bag protecting him, okay?

On it!

SOON:

So now you're up to speed with everything that's happened with us so far!

Thank you, Jake.

Hey, don't mention it.

Guys! Princesses! Vampire Queen! I know how we can beat the Lich!!

It's like Abraham Lincoln once said in the past and also on Mars! I just have to believe in myself. We just have to believe in ourselves! In ALL of our selves!!

What does that even MEAN, Finn?

WE WORK TOGETHER! HOLD ON! USUALLY IT'S EASIER FOR ME TO TALK IF I'M NOT SHOUTING ACROSS A VORTEX!

Jake slide, Jake slide / His body gets longer than it is wide

SOON:

We all have our special skills, right? We should attack together! Look at us: **I'M** good at punches; Princess Bubblegum's super smart; Jake can take the shape of anything he can imagine--

Heh. Yeah.

--Desert Princess can make sand people; Marceline, you're a real-life vampire; Ice King can make giant ice cubes to hold people in--

There's more to me than just my ice powers, Finn. I hope you one day realize that.

And Lumpy Space Princess, you...well, um, you can--

Oh my glob, Finn, it's **SUPER** obvious, I should just bite him. You know, give him a case of the Lumps.

LSP, that's **PERFECT!** As soon as he gets lumpy he won't care about destroying us anymore!

But how can we attack him all at once when he can control our minds? We don't have enough anti-mind-control gems for everybody.

We...

...form...

...TEAMS!!

Some people say they prefer working alone to working in groups, but I bet that's just because they've never had Finn propose a team to them before!

AWESOME:

It's been a sl-**ICE!**

Man, that didn't make sense. You're not even attacking with a sword!

Oh wait, I get ittttttttttttttttttttt

You want some science in your face??

It appears he didn't want science in **OR** about his face, Princess.

Hey Lich! Looks like you've got to **TAKE YOUR LUMPS!**

Oh my glob that's **SO** racist.

OW! He's just skin and bones and I lumpin' bit myself!!

Like I need more lumpin' **LUMPS!**

My crown protects me from the Lich's mind control! Mine too!

High five? If I high five you, will you try to kidnap me?

Ye-um, I mean, uh...there's one way to find out?

We're not making much progress here, Finn. We're running out of time.

The Lich said he'd suck everything up and then throw it into the sun. So, uh, how long do you think that would take?

I've done fun science experiments that suggest the sun is at least a hundred and fifty billion decaquads away.

How much is that, Peebles?

Well, it's a lot of decaquads.

We've managed to keep the Lich too busy fighting us to finish the job...for now. But if he does throw us into the sun it should take us at least a couple of years to get there, unless he can somehow throw us mad nutty hard. But to get such force levels you'd need to--

Oh great, that's plenty of time then!

Yes--except the closer we get to the sun, the hotter things will get. It won't take long for it to be too hot for us to survive!

How long until it's too hot for sweet hats?

I'm gonna say..."soon."

gasp

Three things. One: this isn't working. Two: I don't know how much longer we can keep this up. Three: that guy is the worst.

HOW! COME! WE!

KEEP NOT WINNING?!

Everyone's landing in the same place because now they have the power of *TEAMS* to keep them together. Teamwork is the real power! It's about 1.5 joules per second; ask any scientist!

SOON:

Alright everybody, new plan: we form one giant **SUPER ULTIMATE TEAM** instead! Desert Princess, I need you to make all the Sand Finns **AND** Sand Jakes you can. I want a Sand Bro Army!

Yes sir! I could also make sand Liches, sand witches, and sandwiches if you want!

Just the last one, please!

Ice King, you make Snow Finns too! Make all the snow guys you can! They'll be teaming up with the sand ones.

There's not much moisture in the air so it might be tric--

Ice King **DO YOU WANT EVERYONE TO DIE??**

Okay, well no, not really I guess--

Lumpy Space Princess, you'll tell the Sand and Snow Bros what a jerk the Lich is, so they'll **REALLY** want to punch him. They'll be a little slow since they don't have brains, but that'll stop them from being mind-controlled!

That's easy, 'cause I've got lots of stories about him that you don't even know. I mean, that guy tried to mess up my **RELATIONSHIPS**.

Princess Bubblegum, you'll stay here to organize the army and make sure they go in on my mark. Marceline, you're tough and awesome, so you keep fighting the Lich while we get ready in here.

Not a problem.

What about me, Finn? Isn't there something ol' Jake gets to do?

Yes. My friend, you've got the **MOST IMPORTANT JOB OF ALL!!** And here it is!

Pss Pss Pss Pss Pss Pss Pss

Hee hee! That tickles!

Cool plan though.

Lumpy Space Princess is secretly really happy here because she got the task of spreading gossip around to a bunch of people. That's BASICALLY her dream job!

SOON:

This is really appealing to me for some reason.

I know what you mean, dude.

And then he calls me "talky," and it's like, YEAH, at least I've got something worth saying!!

Looks like we're ready here, Finn.

Alright. Put your gem on, Jake.

Oh, it's ON.

Ha, I didn't even mean that in the "let's go fight" sense! It totally works though.

Heh. Crazy.

I've ordered the first wave of Elemental Finns and Jakes to follow you in, Finn!

Perfect! We're going in!!

Marceline! Remember you promised to give me back my crown in one piece!

Don't get hurt.

Good luck or whatever, Finn. I mean it. I'm being serious.

And good luck, Mr. Jake.

And good luck, M--

And Ice King? Good luck to Ice King? Hello?

See ya Princesses!

You suck me in your bag, man, you know I'm coming back!

If I were you right now I'd have anxiety ATTACKS!

You dumb to do something again, expectin' different things to happen!

The only thing that changed is that we all just started RAPPIN'!

We're gonna end this soon, Lich.

So don't you even blink!

We're gonna see what happens when I...

NO! NO!!

...start to...

...SHRINK!

RIIIIP

EARTH:

Hey. Thanks for keeping The Lich busy while we fought him, sand and ice Finns and Jakes.

Hey, um...was the planet always shaped like that?

Hopefully, dude!!

Listen, we should get back down there. I think there're still some problems that need fixing.

I agree. You two are with me.

Wooooosh!

Wooooosh!

Stop making wooshy noises, guys.

Wooooooosh no way this is awesome wooooosh

Princess Bubblegum! What happened?

I was about to ask you the same thing!

Did you get him?

Well, I GUESS you could say The Lich should've worn a wide-brimmed hat today, because he's spending an awful lot of time...

IN THE SUN.

Yes, we got him. We were lucky to escape ourselves.

Thank you, Marceline. We all owe each of you a debt of gratitude.

Here, thanks for lending me your hat.

Marceline! It's a ROYAL CROWN.

BUMP

So listen, what's with all the dirt everywhere?

BEHIND THE SCENES FACT: All of Adventure Time, the show *AND* the comic, was leading up to Finn's pun in panel three. *ALL OF IT.*

I have no idea! But it's all over the Candy Kingdom.

Weird! When we were hanging out in **SPACE ITSELF**, everything looked all deserty and desertlicious from there too.

Are you saying the sand covers the entire **PLANET?!**

I think so? Probably? I guess?

Oh no!

When the bag broke, we all ended up back where we started. But that desert kingdom was already there in the bag before we showed up!

So?

So the bag changed it somehow! Instead of ending up wherever it started, it ended up on top of us. On top of **EVERYTHING!**

Does Desert Princess know anything about this?

Nobody's seen her since the bag exploded!

Jake and I accept your quest, Princess! We will find Desert Princess and restore this land to its rightful, non-sandy state!

Aw, man! Dude.

We just got back, dude.

Can you restore the Breakfast Kingdom too? All the breakfast citizens have sand in them. It's gross.

Yes! We'll restore **ALL** the kingdoms!

Aw man! **THAT'S EVEN MORE WORK THAN THE FIRST QUEST!**

SOON:

Look man, I appreciate what you're going for, but we can solve this without finding Desert Princess. You know how you get rid of sand?

How?

You wash it off, silly!

Look, all we need to do is take each candy kingdom citizen, like so...

And take a nice bucket of water, like so...

And then dunk one in the other!

Like so! See?

This is **WAY EASIER** than trying to find princesses, Finn.

Man, you dissolved my butt! Now my head is all that's left, and that looks like a butt too!

Butts to this!!

I don't think Desert Princess is responsible for this, Jake. I think it was an accident.

I guess you still wanna find her though, huh?

Hmm...If I were a princess, where would I be hiding?

Hmmm...

"I'm the new princess in town! I'm super nice and everybody likes me! I sure hope I don't get kidnapped by the--"

ICE KING!!

THE ICE KINGDOM:

But I'm super nice and everybody likes me! Why are you doing this?

Because I want you to marry me!

I already politely declined your first offer!

Well I thought about it and I decided you should say "yes" instead!

I just assumed I was seeing things! The sand goes on forever, Finn. There's got to be enough there to...

...to fill in a giant hole?!

...I was gonna say "feed an army" but sure.

WAIT, THAT'S IT! All we have to do is take all the sand covering the world and stick it in that giant hole!

Yes, Jake?

How are we gonna do that, dude? The planet is huge and there's sand everywhere!

I have an idea, Mr. Finn!

What if I used some sand to make a sand version of...myself? Then Sand Me could make another Sand Me, and so on!

Then they all just walk into the hole and jump in!

I've never done a sand version of myself before, but it should work. Right?

SOON:

Okay, this area's clean now, and there's a wave of me making more me spreading across the surface of the planet. That'll take care of the sand, Mister Finn!

Perfect!

ATTENTION, DESERT PRINCESSES!

Wait, hold on a second.

Should it be "Desert Princesses" or "Deserts Princess"?

I dunno, man. I think it's the first one.

Nice. Thanks.

ATTENTION, DESERT PRINCESSES! WALK EAST UNTIL YOU FIND A GIANT HOLE, OKAY? THEN JUMP IN AND FILL IT UP WITH SAND, OKAY? SOUND GOOD?

WHAT IF WE DON'T WANT TO DO THAT THOUGH?

Hello, I'm Desert Princess!

Hah, we're both saying the same thing at the same time!

I like your name!!

WHAT IF--AND THIS IS EMBARRASSING BUT, WELL, WHAT IF WE ALL HAVE A BIT OF A CRUSH ON YOU, FINN?

You guys!! Don't say that!

BUT IT'S TRUE.

AND WE DON'T WANT TO DISAPPEAR WITHOUT GETTING ONE LITTLE FINN KISS.

Oh my gosh oh my gosh this is so embarrassing!

But I can't kiss all of you! There's way too many. I'll get all puckered out!

NOT A PROBLEM, MISTER FINN.

Welp, I'm out. That's my limit of crazy for today!

Um... ha ha

SOON:

Filling in that hole has given us a whole new land to explore! You've literally given us a larger planet to live on, Finn! This is amazing.

Well shoot, Desert Princess did most of the work! I just had to kiss some sand.

Thank you, Desert Princess.

Thank **YOU**, Princess Bubblegum.

Alright! Water Princess, we could use a lake!

You know, I'm really glad I got to meet you, Desert Princess.

I'm--

I'm really glad I got to meet you too, Mister Finn.

Please. All my friends just call me "Finn".

THE END

Drawn by Shelli and Braden

Written by Ryan

Created by Pen

Thanks for reading!

Whoa, check this place out!! And it even comes with a cool creepy bag! I could **TOTALLY** stay here until it's safe outside again.

Actually, I don't--I don't think I like this. It feels weird. It's kinda burning my hand.

Maybe I shouldn't be here after all.

Marcy, I know the mushroom bombs have...changed things. Awakened...things. And I know I've been alone for so long that I've started talking to myself.

But don't be afraid, Marceline! We're tough! We're smart!

We'll make it through this. I promise.

It's fine. There'll be somewhere else to stay. Somewhere else where we can find...friends. Besides, it can't stay like this forever, right?

...

Everything is gonna be fine.

It'll just take some time.

COVER GALLERY

Cover 1A:
Shelli Paroline and Braden Lamb

Covers 1B & 1C:
Chris Houghton
Colors: Kassandra Heller

Cover 1D:
Jeffrey Brown

Emerald City Comicon Exclusive Cover:
Chris Samnee
Colors: Matthew Wilson

San Diego Comic-Con Exclusive Cover:
Pendleton Ward

Annapolis Comic-Con Exclusive Cover:
Sanford Greene

Issue #1 2nd Print:
Chris Houghton
Colors: Kassandra Heller

Issue #1 3rd Print:
Chris Houghton
Colors: Kassandra Heller

Cover 2A:
Chris Houghton
Colors: Kassandra Heller

Cover 2B:
JAB
Colors: Braden Lamb

Cover 2C:
Emily Carroll

Cover 2D:
Becky Dreistadt & Frank Gibson

Issue #2 2nd Print:
Chris Houghton
Colors: Kassandra Heller

Cover 3A:
Chris Houghton
Colors: Kassandra Heller

Cover 3C:
Michael DeForge

Cover 3D:
Stephanie Buscema

Cover 4A:
Chris Houghton
Colors: Kassandra Heller

Cover 4B:
Kassandra Heller

Kassandra HELLER

Cover 4C:
Scott C.

Maine Comic Arts Festival Exclusive:
Melanie Tingdahl
Colors: Lisa Moore

Double Midnight Comics Exclusive:
Mike Holmes
Colors: Lisa Moore

FROM SCRIPT TO PAGE!
BY RYAN NORTH

Above you can see the final page as it appears in ADVENTURE TIME Volume 1 (page 43). I thought I'd show how the script compares to the final page!

In issue one, I wrote out page layouts for Braden and Shelli, saying things like "we've got these panels 1x3 on the page, and then a splashy panel 4, and then panel 5 long and skinny beneath that". But then they surprised me with rough pencils that A) used my layouts in a few cases but B) came up with way better ones a ton of the time. So in this issue (and onwards!) I just said "hey, here are the panels with what's happening inside of them" and let Braden and Shelli do the layouts. They're awesome at it!

PAGE FIVE

Panel 1:
Jake (big) with Finn on his back and DP being pulled up by Finn, as he runs off at full speed. Finn is helping DP up by her hands.
FINN: If we just pick a direction and run, we're bound to hit the edge of the bag eventually!!
DP: Yes!
JAKE: SCIENCE.

Panel 2:
NARRATION: Twenty minutes later:
Jake, flopped out on the ground, exhausted, legs splayed, Finn standing beside him, DP is on her knees in the sand building something.
JAKE: Man, I'm pooped. I don't think running is the answer here, dudes. I think running--I think running might actually be the worst.

Panel 3:
DP has made three sand drinks with straws. She offers the extras to Finn and Jake.
DP: Gentlemen! Maybe we're thinking too two-dimensionally! Maybe we can escape...up?

Panel 4:
We see a low-angle looking up with Finn and DP as Jake spirals off into the sky, legs still on the ground. Finn and DP staring upwards. Finn is taking the offered drink absent-mindedly.
JAKE (words getting smaller as he blasts into the sky): Anything's better than runninggggggggg

Panel 5:
Same angle, but now Finn and DP sip on their sand drinks while they stare at Jake going up into the sky.

Panel 6:
Same angle, but now Finn tastes what he's drinking and spits out sand while DP continues to sip and stare upwards at Jake.

ALT: a little tiny comic at the bottom of the page featuring Marceline, addressing the camera.
P1: Remember when the Lich was attacking me and my totally sweet house?
P2: Remember how instead of helping me out, you turned the page and read about Finn and Jake instead?
p3: Well I don't have to remember because he's still attacking me and IT'S HAPPENING RIGHT NOW!!

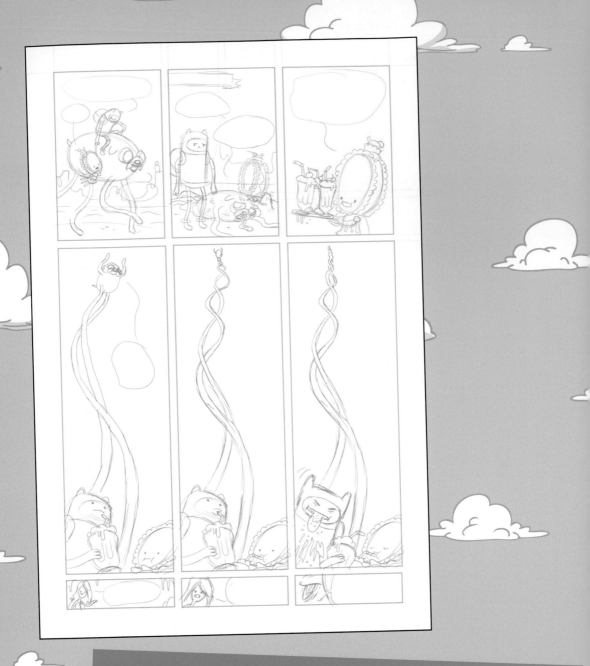

For example, check out the long, tall panels they drew on this page! They work SO WELL and communicate the heights that Jake's reaching up to in a really nice visual way. But it's not just layout: in the script I have Jake's "Anything's better than runninggggggg" line happen in panel 4, but here in the comic his dialogue is spread out across panels 5 and 6 too, being pulled up with Jake as he stretches himself higher. Nice! It makes the page more fun to look at (and read!) and we get the sense of Jake's words fading away as he gets higher up, which is exactly what I was going for. It's always awesome when you can translate vocal effects like this to a silent, visual medium, and still have them come through like I'm whispering into your ear!

At this point I imagine writing this comic like a game of tennis: I send the ball over the net as hard as I can, confident that the other members of the team will be able to return it, and they do, but every single ball they hit returns as a hunk of solid gold.

DANG. TEAMWORK, YO.

OH MY GLOB!

What the lump! There is an entire awesome collection!

Adventure Time Vol 2

Adventure Time Vol 3

Adventure Time:
Vol. 1 - Mathematical Edition

Adventure Time:
Vol. 2 - Mathematical Edition

Adventure Time:
Playing with Fire

Adventure Time:
Marceline & The Scream Queens

Adventure Time
with Fionna & Cake

Adventure Time: Sugary Shorts

ADVENTURE TIME™, CARTOON NETWORK, the logos, and all related characters and elements are trademarks of and © Cartoon Network. (s13)

On sale now at all good book stores

FREAKIN' AWESOME MAG!

NEW ISSUE EVERY FOUR WEEKS!

Woo! POSTERS!

AHH! GIVEAWAYS!

OOH! COMIC STRIP!

WOW! STORIES!

Ooo PUZZLES!

WOW! FREE GIFT EVERY ISSUE!

For more info on the mag or to subscribe visit
www.titanmagazines.com/atmag

How You Got So SMART

by
David
Milgrim

PUFFIN

For all the geniuses,
large and small.

PUFFIN BOOKS
Published by the Penguin Group: London, New York, Australia, Canada, India,
Ireland, New Zealand and South Africa
Penguin Books Ltd, Registered Offices: 80 Strand, London WC2R 0RL, England

puffinbooks.com

First published in the USA by G. P. Putnam's Sons, a division of Penguin Young Readers Group, 2010
Published in Great Britain in Puffin Books 2012
001 – 10 9 8 7 6 5 4 3 2 1

Text and illustrations copyright © David Milgrim, 2010
All rights reserved
The moral right of the author/illustrator has been asserted

Made and printed in China

ISBN: 978–0–718–19737–7

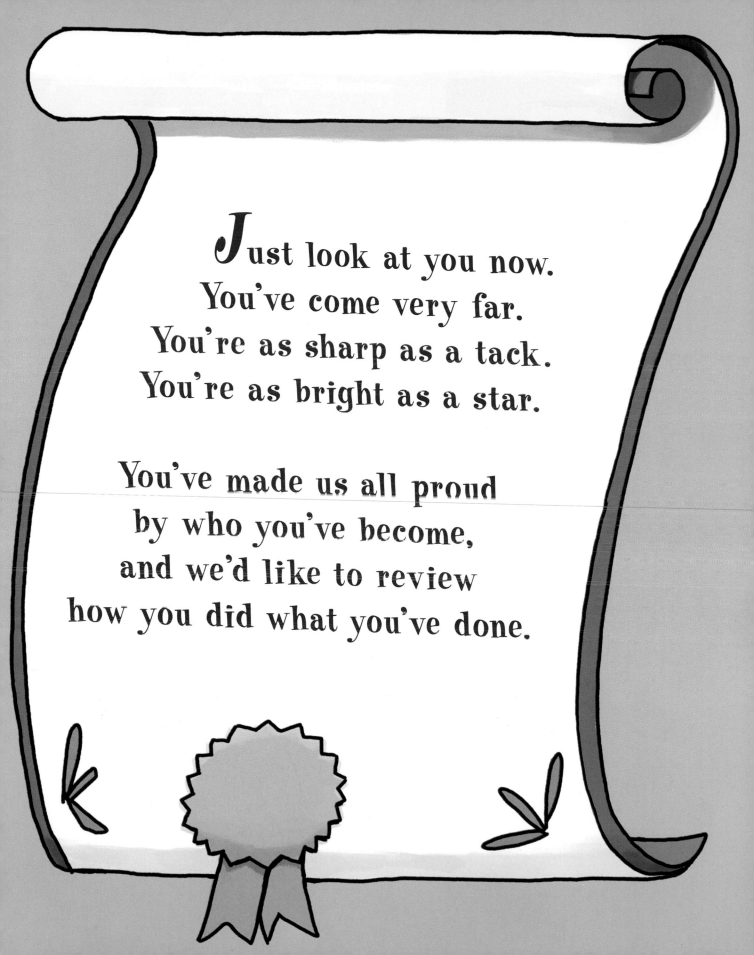

Just look at you now.
You've come very far.
You're as sharp as a tack.
You're as bright as a star.

You've made us all proud
by who you've become,
and we'd like to review
how you did what you've done.

You watched the world closely.

You studied the sounds.

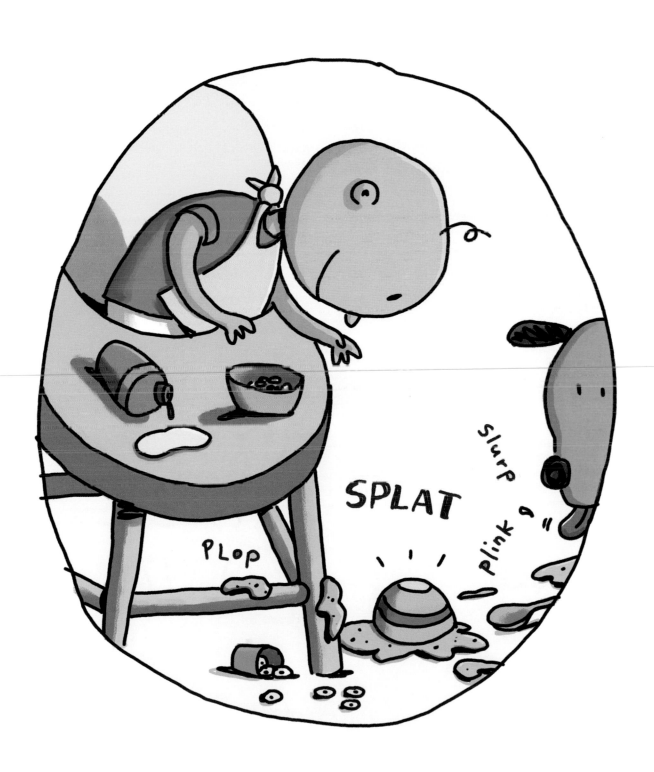

You had a small taste

of whatever you found.

You wandered and wondered.
You loved to explore.

For every answer you got,
you had three questions more.

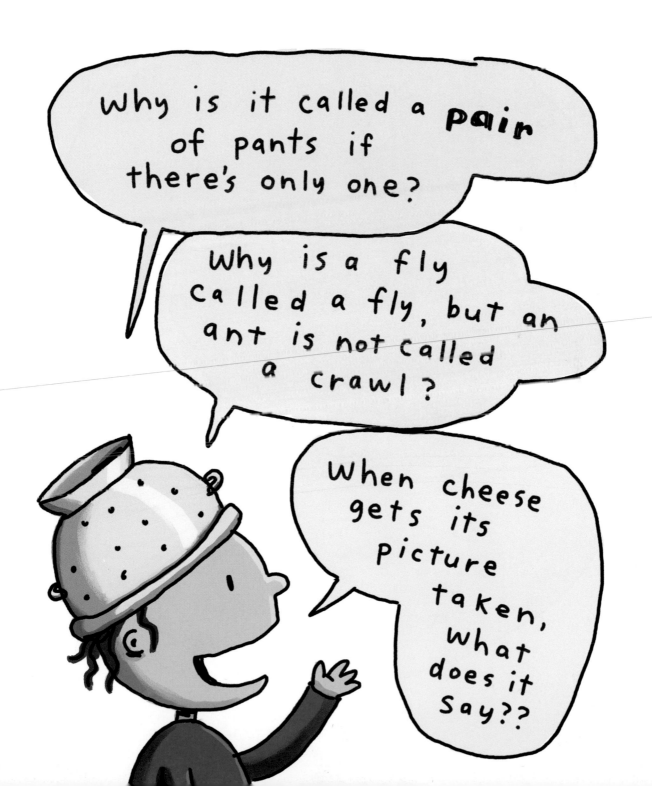

You loved a good mystery.

You prodded and poked.

You made a few friends.
You learned how to share.

You were never afraid
to show that you care.

You gave things a try.
You were brave and courageous.

You liked to do things
that were wild and outrageous.

You loved to be challenged.
You wanted to fly.

The more that you failed,
the harder you tried.

You put things together
to see what they made.

When life gave you lemons,
you made lemonade.

You learned it's okay
if you cry when you're sad

and how to express yourself
when you are mad.

You had many teachers.
You learned from them well.

You had your own stories
you needed to tell.

You played your own music.
You sang with your heart.

And look at you now . . .
you're so brilliantly smart.

You got where you're going.
You did it your way.

Dear Imagination Library Graduate,

My, how time flies. It seems it was only yesterday when your family and friends read you your first story. You were just a baby. Now you're five years old and have grown so much. How exciting!

Although this is your last book from my Imagination Library, you have to promise me you will keep on reading. Every book is a treasure and every time you open one up you will meet new friends and take wonderful journeys to magical places.

You and all of your friends are very special. There is no limit to what you can do or how far you can go. Just remember the lessons my family taught me - dream big dreams; learn everything you can learn; and care for all of those who care for you. You do all of these things and you can be anyone you want to be.

You are terrific and remember...

I Will Always Love You,

Dolly